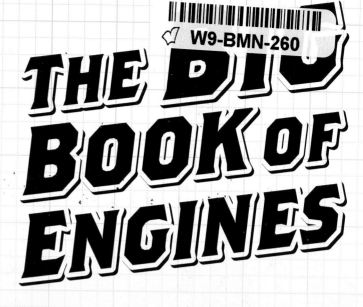

THOMAS & FRIENDS™

THE BIG BOOK OF ENGINES

📖 A GOLDEN BOOK · NEW YORK

Thomas the Tank Engine & Friends™

CREATED BY BRITT ALLCROFT

Based on The Railway Series by The Reverend W Awdry.
© 2014 Gullane (Thomas) LLC.
Thomas the Tank Engine & Friends and Thomas & Friends are trademarks of Gullane (Thomas) Limited.
HIT and the HIT Entertainment logo are trademarks of HIT Entertainment Limited.
All rights reserved. Published in the United States by Golden Books, an imprint of Random House Children's Books, a division of
Random House LLC, 1745 Broadway, New York, NY 10019, and in Canada by Random House of Canada Limited, Toronto, Penguin
Random House Companies. Golden Books, A Golden Book, A Big Golden Book, the G colophon, and the distinctive gold spine are
registered trademarks of Random House LLC.
randomhouse.com/kids   www.thomasandfriends.com
ISBN 978-0-307-93131-3
Printed in the United States of America
10 9 8 7 6 5 4 3 2 1
Random House Children's Books supports the First Amendment and celebrates the right to read.

THOMAS
the Tank Engine™

NO1 ENGINE
est 1945
ON TRACK AND ON TIME

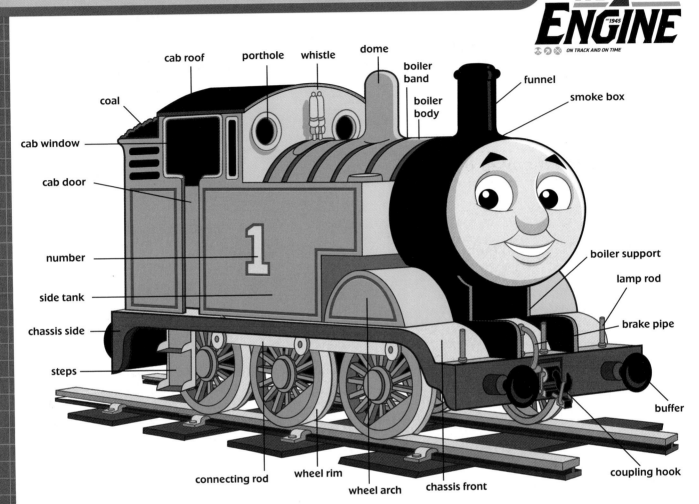

- cab roof
- porthole
- whistle
- dome
- boiler band
- funnel
- boiler body
- smoke box
- coal
- cab window
- cab door
- number
- side tank
- chassis side
- steps
- boiler support
- lamp rod
- brake pipe
- buffer
- coupling hook
- connecting rod
- wheel rim
- wheel arch
- chassis front

All About Thomas

Thomas the Tank Engine is the number 1 engine on the Island of Sodor. He is a cheeky little engine who always tries his best to be Really Useful. He is very proud of his two coaches, Annie and Clarabel, and loves working with them on his own branch line.

One of the kindest engines on Sir Topham Hatt's Railway, Thomas has friends wherever he puffs. People and engines are always pleased to hear the **"Peep! Peep!"** of Thomas' whistle.

Thomas loves to race. His most famous race was against Bertie the Bus. Thomas won, but only just. He also once raced backward against Diesel!

Really Useful Facts

Number: 1

Paintwork: Blue with red boiler bands

Wheels: 6

Steam or diesel engine? Steam

Coaches: Annie and Clarabel

Best friend: Percy

Thomas loves: Pulling passengers up and down his very own branch line

Thomas is a member of the Steam Team!

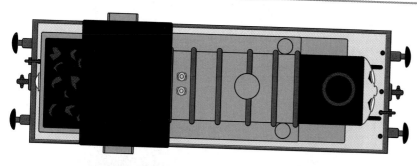

Look and see! Can you spot Thomas' 6 boiler bands, 4 buffers, and 2 whistles?

BUST MY BUFFERS!

When Thomas filled his tank with water from the river, a fish swam into it by accident!

Turn page to read about **Edward**

EDWARD
the Blue Engine

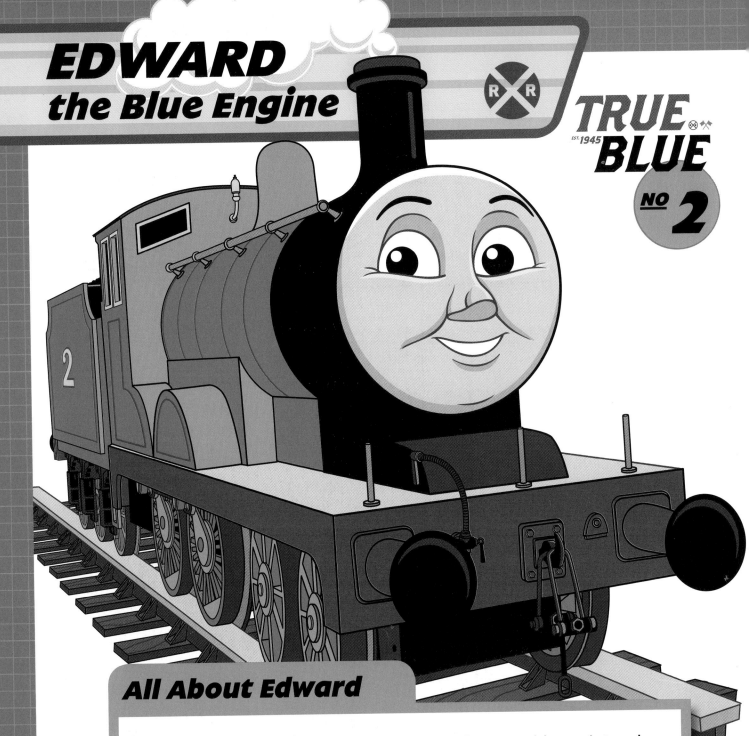

All About Edward

Edward is a fine and steady engine. He has the same blue paintwork with red stripes as Thomas. Edward is a mixed-traffic engine, which means that he can pull coaches or freight—he's as happy pulling passengers as he is working with the Troublesome Trucks!

Although he's not as big as Gordon or Henry, Edward is a Really Useful Engine. Sir Topham Hatt trusts wise Edward to help other engines when they find themselves in trouble.

Edward has his own branch line, which goes from Brendam Dock to Wellsworth.

Really Useful Facts

Number: 2

Paintwork: Blue with red boiler bands

Tender? Yes

Wheels: Edward has 8 wheels and his tender has 6.

Steam or diesel engine? Steam

Edward pulls: Trucks, freight, and passengers

Friends: Gordon and Henry

Edward loves: Pulling passengers on his very own branch line

Edward is a member of the Steam Team!

Number fun!

Count **8** wheels on Edward and find the number **2** on his tender.

BUST MY BUFFERS!

Some engines thought Edward was old and slow until they saw him beat Spencer in a race!

Turn page to read about **Henry**

HENRY
the Green Engine

NO 3

All About Henry

Henry is a big tender engine who loves to go really fast up and down the main line.

Henry used to need special coal, until Sir Topham Hatt sent him to be mended and he was given a new shape and firebox.

One rainy day, Henry went into a tunnel and wouldn't come out! He was afraid that the rain would spoil his fine green paint. Henry finally came out to help Gordon when he burst a safety valve. Now the tunnel is known as "Henry's Tunnel."

Really Useful Facts

Number: 3

Paintwork: Green with red boiler bands

Tender? Yes

Wheels: Henry has 10 wheels and his tender has 6.

Steam or diesel engine? Steam

Henry pulls: Trucks, freight, and passengers

Friends: Gordon and James

Henry loves: Nothing more than his fine green paint!

Henry is a member of the Steam Team!

Spot the Differences

These pictures of Henry look the same, but there are 3 differences between them. Can you spot them all?

① ②

Answers: In picture 2, Henry's steps have turned red, his number 3 is upside down, and his buffers are a different shape.

BUST MY BUFFERS!

Henry was surprised one day when a circus elephant came trumpeting out of a tunnel!

Turn page to read about **Gordon**

All About Gordon

Gordon the Big Express Engine is one of Sir Topham Hatt's biggest and most powerful engines. It is no surprise, then, that Gordon is the fastest on the Steam Team, too. Although he can be boastful, Gordon is hardworking and strong.

Gordon has a very steep hill named after him near Maron Station. You can tell Gordon from the other blue engines because his buffers are a different shape. Gordon's favorite job is to pull the Express down the main line.

Sir Topham Hatt sometimes asks Gordon to pull heavy goods, but Gordon prefers passenger trains. His most famous passenger was the Queen, who came to Sodor on a Royal Visit. Gordon has visited King's Cross Station in London, too!

Really Useful Facts

Number: 4

Paintwork: Blue with red boiler bands

Tender? Yes

Wheels: Gordon has 12 wheels and his tender has 6.

Steam or diesel engine? Steam

Gordon pulls: Passengers and heavy goods

Friends: Henry and James

Gordon loves: Thundering down the line with the Express!

Gordon is a member of the Steam Team!

Odd One Out

One of these Gordons is different from the rest. Can you spot the odd one out?

ⓐ ⓑ ⓒ ⓓ ⓔ

Answer: d. His whistle is missing.

BUST MY BUFFERS!

Gordon once got stuck in a ditch on purpose so he wouldn't have to pull a freight train!

Turn page to read about **James**

JAMES
the Red Engine

NO 5

Red Engine

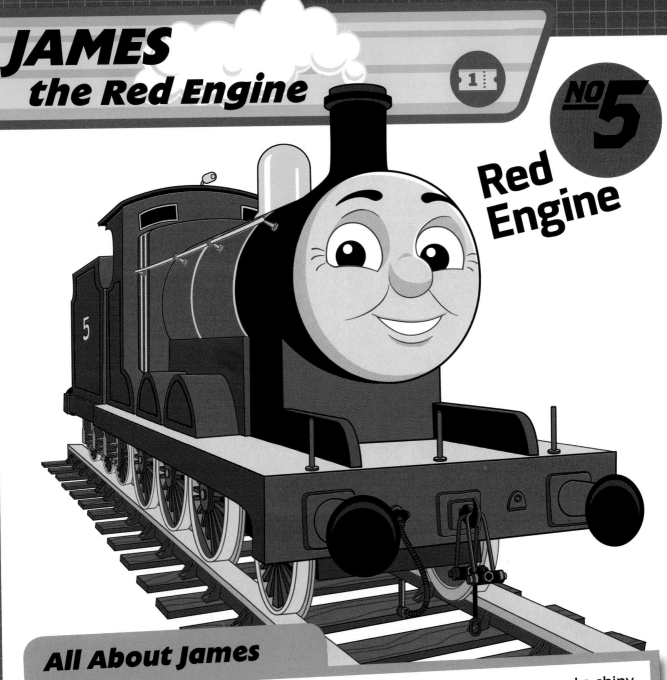

All About James

James is a medium-sized tender engine with a coat of scarlet paint and a shiny brass dome. James likes to think of himself as a Really Splendid Engine, and his boasting sometimes gets him in trouble.

When he first came to Sodor, James was painted black. He had wooden brake blocks, too, which caught fire! When his brakes were mended, James was painted red. He loves to keep his shiny coat clean and often complains if he has to pull dirty trucks.

One of James' favorite jobs is to pull the Express when Gordon is away. Although his wheels aren't as big as Gordon's, James can go at high speed, too.

Really Useful Facts

Paintwork: Red with gold boiler bands

Tender? Yes

Wheels: James has 8 wheels and his tender has 6.

Steam or diesel engine? Steam

James pulls: Coaches – he hates pulling trucks!

Best friends: Tender engines Gordon and Henry

James loves: His red paintwork and shiny brass dome

James is a member of the Steam Team!

Ticket to Ride

Find 5 tickets hidden in this picture of James.

Answer: The tickets are hidden in James' dome, on his buffer and tender, on his face, and above his wheel.

When James' brake pipe once broke, a passenger had to give up his bootlace to mend it!

Turn page to read about **Percy**

PERCY
the Small Engine

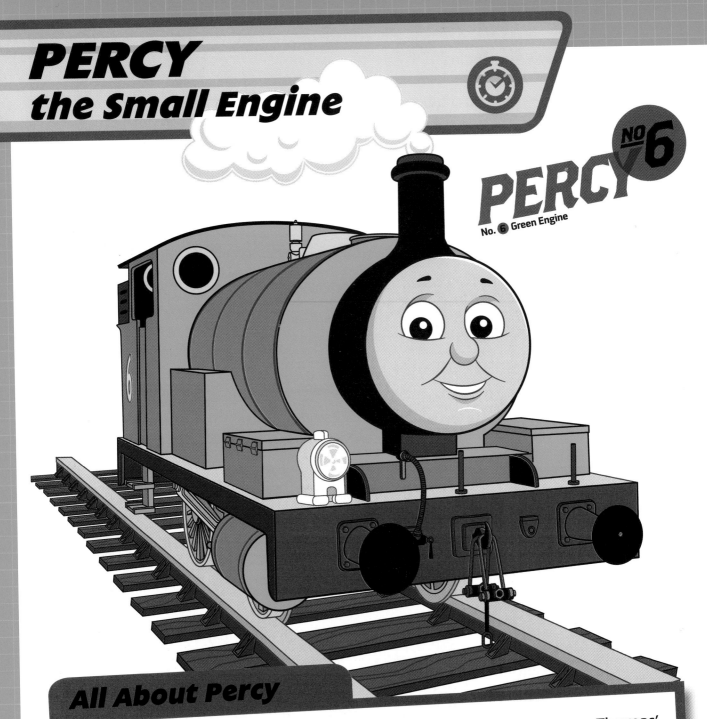

PERCY No 6
No. 6 Green Engine

All About Percy

Percy is a cheeky green saddle tank who was brought to Sodor to run Thomas' branch line during the big engines' strike.

Although Percy is a small engine, he often likes to play jokes on Gordon and James to put them in their place.

Since he arrived on the island, Percy has had a lot of accidents—he has crashed into some buffers, a chocolate factory, the sea, and a truck of molasses!

When he's not pulling trucks, Percy can be seen pulling the mail train, taking Annie and Clarabel when Thomas is busy, or working in the yard at Ffarquhar.

Really Useful Facts

Number: 6

Paintwork: Green with red boiler bands

Tender? No

Wheels: 4

Steam or diesel engine? Steam

Percy pulls: Trucks, the mail train, and passengers

Best friend: Thomas

Percy loves: Playing tricks on engines, even if they're bigger than him

Percy is a member of the Steam Team!

Going Green

Percy is a green engine. Check the other engines that are green.

- ✓ **Henry**
- ☐ **Rosie**
- ✓ **Oliver**
- ✓ **Duck**

Answer: Henry, Oliver, and Duck are green engines, too!

BUST MY BUFFERS!

Percy once wore a scarf around his funnel! He crashed into a trolley on his line, and Sir Topham Hatt's pants became wrapped around his funnel.

Turn page to read about **Toby**

TOBY
the Tram Engine

bell

porthole

lamp

wooden panels

sideplate

coupling hook

cowcatcher

All About Toby

Toby is an old-fashioned steam tram engine with gray cowcatchers that cover his wheels. You can often find him cheerfully working on the quarry line with his faithful coach, Henrietta.

Some engines make fun of Toby because of his shape, but Toby doesn't mind being square!

Toby was saved from the junkyard by a stout gentleman who brought him to work on his own railway. Can you guess who it was? That's right: Sir Topham Hatt! Toby didn't want to leave Henrietta behind, so she came with him to work on the Island of Sodor.

Toby is proud to be the number 7 engine in the Steam Team.

Really Useful Facts

Number: 7

Paintwork: Brown—Toby is made of wood.

Wheels: 6—they are hidden under his sideplates.

Tender? No

Steam or diesel engine? Steam

Coach: Henrietta

Toby pulls: Trucks, freight, and passengers

Friends: Flora and Mavis

Toby loves: Ringing his bell to let everyone know he is coming!

Toby is a member of the Steam Team!

Shadow Match

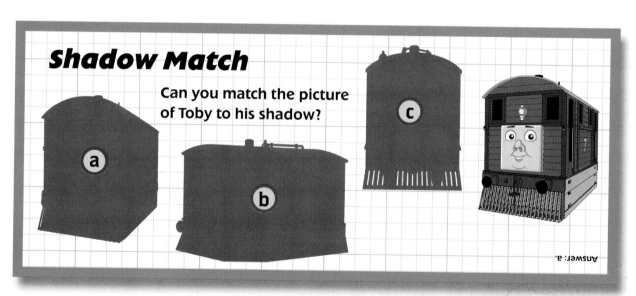

Can you match the picture of Toby to his shadow?

a

b

c

Answer: a.

BUST MY BUFFERS!

For a long time, Toby was the only tram engine on the Island of Sodor—then Flora steamed into town!

Turn page to read about **Emily**

EMILY

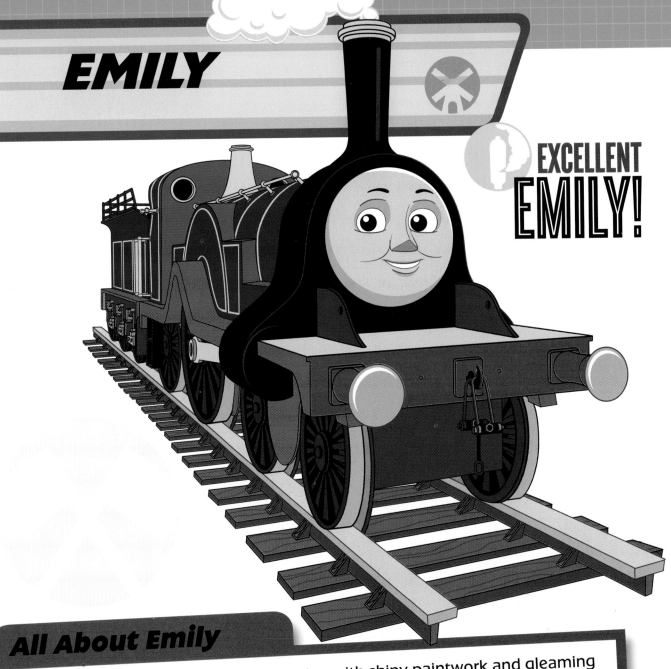

EXCELLENT EMILY!

All About Emily

Emily is a beautiful emerald-green engine with shiny paintwork and gleaming brass fittings.

She can be a little bossy and thinks that she knows best, but she is always ready to help a friend. She is the newest member of the Steam Team.

Before Emily got her own coaches, she pulled Annie and Clarabel—but Thomas did not like that! Sir Topham Hatt gave her two coaches as a reward for saving Oliver from an accident.

It is easy to tell Emily apart from other engines because of her two big driving wheels and shiny brass safety valve cover.

Really Useful Facts

Paintwork: Dark green with gold boiler bands

Tender? Yes

Wheels: Emily has 8 wheels and her tender has 6.

Steam or diesel engine? Steam

Emily pulls: Mostly passengers but sometimes trucks

Friends: Thomas and Oliver

Emily loves: Finishing her jobs on time

Emily is a member of the Steam Team!

Spot the Differences

These pictures of Emily look the same, but there are 3 differences between them.

②

①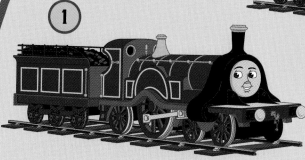

Can you spot them all?

Answers: In picture 2, the paintwork on Emily's tender has changed, and one of her portholes and her coupling hook are missing.

BUST MY BUFFERS!

Emily once thought she saw a monster at Black Loch, but it was really just a friendly seal.

Turn page to read about all Thomas' other **friends**

ANNIE and CLARABEL

All About Annie and Clarabel

Annie and Clarabel are Thomas' faithful coaches and the most famous carriages on the Island of Sodor. Although they are a little old-fashioned, Thomas wouldn't be without them on his branch line.

You can tell them apart by their names painted on their sides. While Annie carries only passengers, Clarabel has two compartments, one for passengers and the other for luggage and a guard. Annie is always the first coach pulled by Thomas, and she travels facing him. Clarabel always travels behind Annie, facing away from Thomas.

Really Useful Facts

Paintwork: Brown

Annie and Clarabel carry: Passengers and luggage

Wheels: 4 each

Friends: Thomas and Percy

They love: Working with Thomas on their branch line

They don't like: When Thomas is being troublesome

BUST MY BUFFERS!

Lots of engines besides Thomas have pulled Annie and Clarabel, including Percy, Toby, Emily, and Stanley.

BASH and DASH

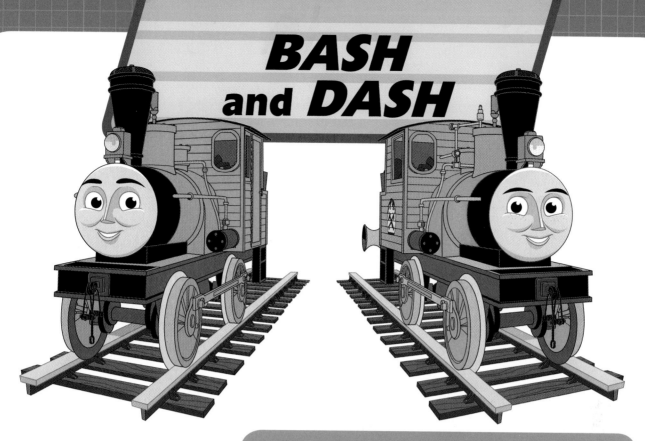

All About Bash and Dash

Bash and Dash are small twin engines who like to finish each other's sentences. They used to work on the railway on the mainland, but they caused too much trouble and were sent to help on Misty Island, where they became "Logging Locos," along with Ferdinand.

Really Useful Facts

Paintwork: Golden yellow and gray

Steam or diesel engines? Steam

Wheels: Each engine has 4 wheels

Jobs: Transporting logs made of jobi wood

Best friend: Ferdinand

The twins love: Working together for double the fun!

Bash and Dash are Logging Locos!

BUST MY BUFFERS!

Although they are steam engines, Bash and Dash use oil and wood for fuel!

BELLE

lamp

water cannon

hazard lamp

RIGHT ON TIME

All About Belle

Belle is a big blue engine who looks very sharp with her gold and red paint. She has a loud whistle and a brass bell—everyone knows when Belle is on her way!

Helpful, charming, and full of energy, Belle always gets her jobs done on time. She wants to do her best and be the best. Some of the other engines might be a little bit jealous of Belle if she weren't so nice! As it is, Belle has made lots of new friends since she arrived on Sodor.

Really Useful Facts

Number: 6120

Paintwork: Blue with gold and red trim

Steam or diesel engine? Steam

Wheels: 12

Tender? No

Belle pulls: Mostly trucks and goods trains

Friends: Thomas and Flynn

Belle loves: Her two water cannons, from which she can squirt water to fight fires!

Belle doesn't like: Finishing her jobs late—being Really Useful is very important for Belle.

BUST MY BUFFERS!

Belle's not a fire engine, but she can fight fires in a pinch! Her paintwork makes her look a bit like Hank.

BERTIE
the Bus

All About Bertie

An old-fashioned red single-decker passenger bus, **Bertie** is loved by his passengers and is proud of the splendid service he provides. Bertie knows that he must not be late bringing passengers to the station or they will miss their trains!

Really Useful Facts

Paintwork: Red

Fuel: Diesel

Wheels: 4

Jobs: Transporting passengers around the island

Friends: Thomas and Edward

Bertie loves: Teasing the engines because they have to travel on tracks!

Bertie doesn't like: Waiting at traffic lights and in jams

Bertie's most famous adventure was when he and Thomas had a Great Race. Although Bertie lost, the two have been firm friends ever since. When Thomas got stuck in a snowdrift, cheerful Bertie took Thomas' passengers home.

BUST MY BUFFERS!

Did you know that Thomas and Bertie had a second race? This time Bertie won, because Thomas had to stop and collect medals for the schoolchildren.

BILL and BEN

All About Bill and Ben

Bill and Ben are twin engines who work for the Sodor China Clay Company. They have the letters "SCC" on their sides and "Brendam Bay" above their faces. The only way you can tell them apart is by their nameplates—they are exactly the same in every other way!

Little Bill and Ben are cheeky and rather troublesome—they love to play tricks on engines who are much bigger than they are. Edward is one of the only engines who can keep them in order.

Bill and Ben don't carry passengers or have coaches. You'll find them at the quarry, at the docks, or busy working on Edward's branch line.

Really Useful Facts

Paintwork: Dark yellow with red buffer beams

Tenders? No

Wheels: Each engine has 4 wheels.

Steam or diesel engines? Steam

The twins pull: Trucks of China Clay at the quarry near Brendam

Friends: Mavis and Edward

The twins love: Playing pranks on bigger engines!

Bill and Ben are saddle tank engines, like Percy, and are known as the "Claypit Twins."

BULSTRODE
the Barge

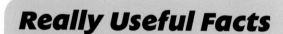

funnel

lifesaver

stern

starboard side

rudder

port side

hull

bow

BULSTRODE

All About Bulstrode

Sulky **Bulstrode** is an old motorized Sea Barge who worked at the harbor on the Island of Sodor. He used to carry coal, stone, and other cargo but always complained rudely about being loaded too slowly.

One day Percy caused an accident by pushing a row of trucks off a dock and damaging Bulstrode's hull — and sinking him! The trucks said that it served Bulstrode right because he was always causing trouble and blaming them for his own mistakes.

Bulstrode was saved and towed to Knapford Beach, where he was turned into a children's playground. Children love to play on him all day!

BUST MY BUFFERS!
Bulstrode would like to be refloated and be Really Useful again!

Really Useful Facts

Paintwork: Dark gray with a red bottom

Fuel: Bulstrode doesn't need fuel now, as he doesn't go anywhere!

Wheels: No wheels, but he has 3 tires on each side of his deck to help buffer the edges of his hull.

Jobs: He used to carry heavy loads of rock, but now he's a playground.

Friends: Bulstrode doesn't have many friends because he is so grumpy!

Bulstrode loves: Being out on the sea

CAPTAIN
the Lifeboat

mast

lifesaver

oar

All About Captain

Captain is a wooden rescue boat who works at the Sodor Search and Rescue Center. A cheerful hero, he always stays calm in an emergency. He never makes a fuss about doing his job—if someone's in trouble, Captain will always come to the rescue.

Captain loves being the "sea" part of the rescue team. With Rocky the Rescue Crane on rails and Harold the Helicopter circling in the skies, everyone on Sodor can feel safe with this brave trio looking out for them.

Really Useful Facts

Paintwork: Yellow, blue, and red with a white stripe

Fuel: Diesel

Jobs: Rescuing people and other boats out at sea

Friends: Harold, Rocky, and Salty

Captain loves: Powering through the waves on rescue missions

Captain doesn't like: People making a fuss—he's a quiet hero.

BUST MY BUFFERS!

Captain has his very own lifeboat shed at the Sodor Search and Rescue Center, from which he launches into the water.

CHARLIE

All About Charlie

Cheeky **Charlie** is a small and playful engine from the mainland who likes to have a lot of fun. He is always ready for an adventure and sometimes forgets he has work to do before he can go off and play.

Really Useful Facts

Number: 14

Paintwork: Purple with gold trim and red wheels

Steam or diesel engine? Steam

Wheels: 6

Charlie pulls: Trucks

Friends: Thomas and Percy

Charlie loves: Racing engines and splashing through puddles

While Charlie can be a little mischievous, he's always ready to help out a friend in need. He and Thomas are now good friends, though when they first met, all Charlie wanted to do was race against Thomas!

BUST MY BUFFERS!

Although Charlie is from the mainland, he wears number 14 on Sir Topham Hatt's Railway.

CRANKY
the Crane

LIFT AND **LOAD**

All About Cranky

Cranky is by far the tallest vehicle on the Island of Sodor. He towers above the engines on Sir Topham Hatt's Railway. From high up, he can see all the comings and goings on the island.

Cranky mainly works at the docks and can't move on his own. He can be taken down and transported to other areas of the island in an emergency, but it's a big job for the engines!

Although he looks tough and is rather rude to the engines, Cranky has a kind side, too. Once, he helped Thomas find Percy during a game of "Hide and Peep." Percy was hiding behind a wall and wouldn't come out!

Really Useful Facts

Paintwork: Green

Wheels: None

Steam or diesel crane? Diesel

Jobs: Loading and unloading crates and goods from ships

Friends: Cranky doesn't have many friends because he's so grumpy!

Cranky loves: Being tall and seeing far across Sodor

Cranky doesn't like: Engines — he calls them "little bugs"!

BUST MY BUFFERS!

Once, in a thunderstorm, a ship crashed into the docks and made Cranky topple over! Thomas and Percy rescued him.

DIESEL

All About Diesel

Nicknamed "Devious Diesel" by the other engines, **Diesel** believes that Steamies are no match for diesels. Oily, scheming, and ever ready to stir up trouble in the shed, Diesel doesn't like the steam engines and they don't like him.

Diesel was the very first diesel engine to be brought to Sodor, to help Duck at Brendam. He told the Steamies that Duck had called them rude names, but his lies were found out and Diesel was sent home in disgrace. He later came back when Percy was being repaired.

Diesel is not all bad, though, and given the chance, he can be a Really Useful Engine.

Really Useful Facts

Paintwork: Black with a red buffer beam

Steam or diesel engine? Diesel, of course!

Wheels: 6

Diesel pulls: Trucks

Friends: The Troublesome Trucks, Diesel 10, Iron 'Arry, and Iron Bert

Diesel loves: Stirring up trouble for Steamies!

Diesel doesn't like: Being sent away when he's been naughty

BUST MY BUFFERS!

Diesel has shunted more freight trucks in one day than any other diesel.

DIESEL 10

All About Diesel 10

Diesel 10 is a large, grumpy engine who loves to bully and tease steam engines. He is Sodor's strongest—but not quite largest—diesel.

Diesel 10 has a crane arm on his roof with a metal claw attached called "Pinchy." He uses this claw to lift scrap metal into trucks on Sir Topham Hatt's Railway.

Thomas and Percy used to be frightened of him and made sure to avoid him whenever possible, especially when Diesel 10 called them names like "Teapot" and "Puffball."

One day Diesel 10 chased Thomas and Lady onto an unsafe viaduct, but he was too heavy to cross and the viaduct gave way. Diesel 10 landed on a passing barge below.

Really Useful Facts

Paintwork: Muddy green and yellow

Steam or diesel engine? Very much a diesel

Wheels: 8

Diesel 10 pulls: Trucks and heavy loads

Friends: Diesel

Diesel 10 loves: Causing trouble and showing off his strength

BUST MY BUFFERS!

Diesel 10 was an important engine in helping to construct Sodor Airport. He helped clear the line when a tower collapsed.

DONALD and DOUGLAS

All About Donald and Douglas

This pair of twins arrived from Scotland together, and although Sir Topham Hatt was only expecting one engine, he decided to keep both of them. He gave **Donald** the number 9 and **Douglas** the number 10, and gave them both nameplates with gold writing.

Donald and Douglas are a tricky pair and have swapped nameplates to pretend to be each other! Nevertheless, they are among the most reliable working engines on the island.

If they hadn't come to Sodor, these twin engines would surely have been scrapped. They have found a very happy home on the island.

Really Useful Facts

Paintwork: Black

Tenders? Yes

Number: Donald is 9 and Douglas is 10. They used to be known as 57646 and 57647.

Wheels: 6 each with 6 on their tenders

Steam or diesel engines? Steam

The twins pull: Trucks. They also help repair tracks.

Friends: Duck, Edward, and Oliver

The twins love: Snow! They are excellent wearing snowplows.

BUST MY BUFFERS!

Donald and Douglas were so upset when they crashed into Trevor's hay cart, they didn't talk to each other. Duck had to get them talking again.

DUCK the Great Western Engine

All About Duck

Duck is a medium-sized green engine without a separate tender. He has the letters "GWR" on his side, which stand for "Great Western Railway," where Duck used to work.

Duck came to Sodor to take over Percy's shunting duties when Percy was helping to build Knapford Harbor. Now, with help from Oliver, Duck runs a branch line that runs from Tidmouth to Arlesburgh.

Duck sometimes helps on other lines and is popular with the engines and Sir Topham Hatt, who says that Duck makes everything run like clockwork. All in all, he is a Really Useful Engine!

Really Useful Facts

Paintwork: Green with a red buffer beam

Tender? No

Number: 8

Wheels: 6

Steam or diesel engine? Steam

Duck pulls: Freight and coaches

Friends: Oliver

Duck loves: Pulling passengers on his own branch line

Duck doesn't like: When Diesel tells tall tales about him

BUST MY BUFFERS!

Duck's real name is Montague, but the engines call him "Duck" because they say his uneven wheels make him waddle!

DUNCAN

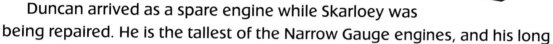

All About Duncan

Duncan is a stubborn engine who works on Sodor's Narrow Gauge Railway in the hills. The Railway is run by Mr. Percival.

Duncan arrived as a spare engine while Skarloey was being repaired. He is the tallest of the Narrow Gauge engines, and his long funnel and high-roofed cab can make tunnels a tight squeeze. He is painted yellow and wears nameplates and the number 6 on his sides.

Duncan is a noisy engine and likes to have something to complain about. He used to rock and roll along the track until this caused a tunnel to collapse on him!

Really Useful Facts

Paintwork: Yellow with gold boiler bands

Tender? No

Number: 6

Wheels: 4

Steam or diesel engine? Steam

Duncan pulls: Coaches

Friends: The Narrow Gauge engines

Duncan loves: Being polished and rocking and rolling!

BUST MY BUFFERS!

Duncan used to be painted red, like Rheneas and Skarloey.

ELIZABETH
the Vintage Wagon

All About Elizabeth

Elizabeth is a vintage Sentinel steam wagon. She was Sir Topham Hatt's first truck, but she was stored in a shed for some time before Thomas found her by accident. She was very pleased to be rescued and was fixed up and made roadworthy again.

Now she works at the quarry with Rusty, where the three-way tipper behind her cab comes in handy for all sorts of jobs.

Although Elizabeth believes that roads are much better than rails, she often helps the engines out. If any cheeky engine tells her she is old, Elizabeth scowls and says, "I'm not old—I'm vintage!"

Really Useful Facts

Paintwork: Maroon with gold and black stripes

Wheels: 4

Doors: 2

Fuel: Gasoline

Friends: Sir Topham Hatt and Thomas

Elizabeth loves: Scolding lazy or rude engines

Elizabeth doesn't like: Being stuck inside—she'd rather be out on the roads all day.

BUST MY BUFFERS!

Sir Topham Hatt first learned to drive in Elizabeth—a long time ago!

FERDINAND

All About Ferdinand

Gentle giant **Ferdinand** is a large steam engine, steady and slow. He works on Misty Island as one of the "Logging Locos" with Bash and Dash. He is built for tough work and dealing with heavy loads rather than speed.

Like little Bash and Dash, Ferdinand runs on wood and oil, and can often be heard saying, "That's right!"

Ferdinand has a splendid coat of turquoise paint, which looks like the water that surrounds Misty Island. The brass lamp next to his funnel is Really Useful for helping Ferdinand see through the mist and in dark tunnels.

Really Useful Facts

Paintwork: Turquoise and gray

Wheels: 8 with 4 on his tender

Steam or diesel engine? Steam

Jobs: Shunting trucks of jobi wood and other heavy loads

Friends: Bash and Dash

Ferdinand loves: Working on beautiful Misty Island

Ferdinand doesn't like: Being stuck in dark tunnels

BUST MY BUFFERS!

Ferdinand can make special tweeting sounds with his whistles!

FLORA
the Steam Tram

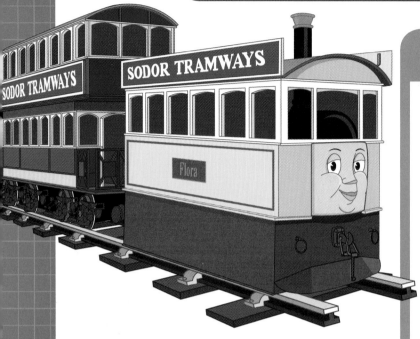

All About Flora

Flora is very proud to be one of only two tram engines on the Island of Sodor that run on steam. Her big double-decker tramcar is her pride and joy.

Flora is painted yellow with green and white lining, red cowcatchers and sideplates, and green boards on her roof reading "Sodor Tramways."

When she first arrived on Sodor, Flora led the Great Waterton Parade with Toby. Thomas thought that his friend Toby would be upset, but he was delighted to meet another tram engine at last!

Flora can travel on tracks or roads, though she likes working on Sir Topham Hatt's Railway with her steam engine friends the most.

Really Useful Facts

Paintwork: Yellow with green stripes, red cowcatchers and sideplates

Wheels: 4

Steam or diesel engine? Steam

Flora pulls: A double-decker tramcar

Best friend: Toby

Flora loves: Being one half of Sodor's steam tram pair!

Flora doesn't like: Upsetting other engines — kind Flora loves engines big and small!

BUST MY BUFFERS!

While Flora runs on standard gauge tracks, she was rebuilt from a narrow gauge.

FLYNN
the Fire Engine

All About Flynn

Flynn is Sodor's very own fire engine and a member of the Sodor Search and Rescue Team. He is bright red and is always ready to race to the rescue.

He can travel by road or rail, which comes in very useful in an emergency. With his two powerful water jets and long ladders, Flynn may look flashy, but he's not one to boast.

Sometimes Flynn can get in a muddle, because he's such a keen and eager fire engine. He tries his best to help anyone in trouble and is a Sodor hero.

Really Useful Facts

Paintwork: Red with yellow stripes

Fuel: Diesel

Wheels: 6 engine wheels and 4 road wheels

Jobs: Putting out fires with his powerful water cannons

Friends: Thomas and Belle

Flynn loves: Putting out fires and keeping people and engines safe

BUST MY BUFFERS!

Flynn carries lots of rescue equipment wherever he goes, including hoses, water jets, ladders, axes, and other tools.

GEORGE
the Steamroller

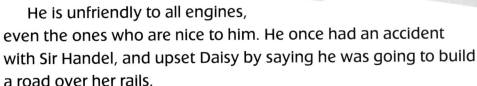

All About George

George is a grumpy green steamroller who is no friend of the engines. He often chants, "Railways are no good! Pull 'em up! Turn 'em into roads!"

He is unfriendly to all engines, even the ones who are nice to him. He once had an accident with Sir Handel, and upset Daisy by saying he was going to build a road over her rails.

After George was careless covering some tracks, causing Thomas to derail, Sir Topham Hatt removed George's roller to teach him a lesson. Now, with his roller back in place, George is much more careful but still enjoys paving over tracks when he gets the chance.

Really Useful Facts

Paintwork: Green

Steam or diesel engine? Steam

Wheels: 3

Jobs: Paving over old railway tracks with his roller

Friends: George doesn't have friends and he doesn't want any!

George loves: Rolling the roads as flat as a pancake!

George doesn't like: Railway tracks—he'd like to pull them up and turn them into roads.

BUST MY BUFFERS!

George's Driver once gave Sir Topham Hatt a ride, but George lost control and rolled into a pool of mud!

HANK

All About Hank

Hank is a big and bold steam engine. He is eager to please and has the strength of a giant.

Hank doesn't look like some of the other steam engines on Sodor, as he has lots of bells and whistles. He came to the island all the way from America!

When Hank first arrived, he made Thomas cross by calling him small, but Thomas quickly realized that Hank means well and has a very big heart.

Unlike some of the bigger engines, Hank is very kind, and is willing to offer help to smaller engines who are struggling with their loads.

Really Useful Facts

Paintwork: Dark blue with red boiler bands and cowcatcher

Tender? Yes

Wheels: Hank has 12 wheels and his tender has 8.

Steam or diesel engine? Steam

Hank pulls: Trucks and heavy freight trains

Friends: Thomas

Hank loves: Blowing his whistle at everyone he passes!

Hank doesn't like: Upsetting other engines

BUST MY BUFFERS!

To celebrate Hank's arrival on Sodor, there was a grand party at Knapford Station!

HAROLD
the Helicopter

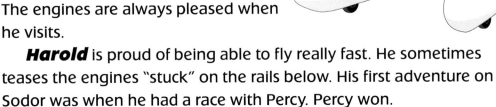

All About Harold

In Sodor's skies you'll hear Harold's whirring blades before you see him. The engines are always pleased when he visits.

Harold is proud of being able to fly really fast. He sometimes teases the engines "stuck" on the rails below. His first adventure on Sodor was when he had a race with Percy. Percy won.

Harold used to work for the coast guard at Dryaw Airfield, keeping a watchful eye over the island in case of trouble. Harold can land on water as well as land, which makes him a Really Useful Machine.

When the Sodor Search and Rescue Center was built, Harold joined the rescue team there, along with Rocky and Captain.

Really Useful Facts

Paintwork: White with a red stripe

Blades: 3

Wheels: 4

Jobs: Patrolling the island on Search and Rescue missions, dropping food to villagers, and spotting damaged tracks

Friends: Percy, Rocky, and Captain

Harold loves: Flying and being in the air

Harold doesn't like: Bad weather, when he has to stay on the ground

BUST MY BUFFERS!

Harold was nicknamed "Whirlybird" by the engines on Sodor.

HIRO

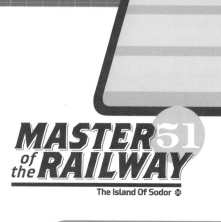

MASTER of the RAILWAY 51
The Island Of Sodor

All About Hiro

Hiro is a wise old tender engine who comes from Japan. He is said to have been the first steam engine on the Island of Sodor, and was nicknamed "The Master of the Railway."

After many good years of service, Hiro started to break down. The Steamworks did not have any spare parts, so Hiro was put in a siding and forgotten about.

Then Thomas made a great discovery and brought engine parts to mend Hiro. Hiro soon looked like a patchwork engine of many colors!

After that, Hiro was taken to the Steamworks and mended properly.

Really Useful Facts

Number: 51

Paintwork: Black with gold bands and fittings and red wheels

Steam or diesel engine? Steam

Wheels: 10 with 8 on his tender

Jobs: Hiro is not a working engine, but sometimes pulls flower trucks.

Hiro loves: Visiting his friends on Sodor

Hiro doesn't like: The Smelters' Yard

BUST MY BUFFERS!

Once, Hiro tried to help give orders for Sir Topham Hatt but made some mistakes and was given the nickname "Master of Muddle"!

IRON 'ARRY and IRON BERT

All About 'Arry and Bert

Iron 'Arry and his brother **Iron Bert** are diesel engines who work down in the Sodor Ironworks and Smelters' Yard. They love breaking up old steam engines, and would really like to melt down Stepney and Oliver if given the chance.

As with most Diesels, 'Arry and Bert feel that diesel engines are better than steam engines. Steamies and Diesels have been known to help each other in times of trouble, but their friendship is quickly forgotten.

Really Useful Facts

Paintwork: Green-gray with yellow hazard stripes on their fronts and rears and yellow cabs. They have "Sodor Ironworks" written on their sides in white.

Steam or diesel engines? Diesel

Wheels: 6 each

Jobs: Melting down scrap at the Smelters' Yard

Friends: Diesel and Diesel 10

'Arry and Bert love: Being naughty and scaring Steamies!

'Arry and Bert don't like: Being told what to do by steam engines . . . or anyone else!

Some of the steam engines call this pair "The Grim Messengers of Doom."

JACK
the Front Loader

All About Jack

Jack is the friendliest front loader the island has ever seen. He and his construction crew work on projects all over Sodor.

He has a bucket at the front and a bucket at the back. Jack loves his job and is eager to please. When he first arrived on Sodor, his job was to clear room for railway lines. Jack worked well but soon ran into trouble trying to do too much. He learned his lesson, and made things better by holding up a collapsing bridge until Thomas had passed over. He hurt his arms, but they were quickly repaired. Jack is now one of the Pack.

Really Useful Facts

Number: 11

Paintwork: Red — the top half of his cab is cream

Wheels: 2 little ones at the front and 2 bigger ones at the back

Jobs: Working for the Sodor Construction Company on building jobs

Jack loves: Being one of the machines in the Pack

BUST MY BUFFERS!

Jack's best friends are Thomas and the rest of the Pack.

JEREMY
the Jet Plane

All About Jeremy

Jeremy is a jolly jet plane who believes that wings are better than wheels!

He enjoys being able to do things that the steam engines can only dream of but chooses to ignore the many things he cannot do that they can!

When push comes to shove, Jeremy forgets his boastfulness and becomes part of the team.

Jeremy is the only plane on the Island of Sodor to have a name.

Really Useful Facts

Paintwork: White with blue paint above his windshield and around his engines

Wheels: 6, which he uses for take-off and landing

Jobs: Working at Sodor Airport

Friend: Thomas

Jeremy loves: Having the freedom of the skies!

Jeremy doesn't like: Storms—because he's not allowed to fly

BUST MY BUFFERS!

Percy once thought that Jeremy was a spaceship in the sky!

KEVIN
the Mobile Crane

All About Kevin

Kevin is a friendly and funny crane who works with Victor at the Sodor Steamworks helping to repair the engines. He hasn't worked there for very long, but he is always ready to lend a helping hook.

Kevin can sometimes drive Victor crazy because he is always dropping engine parts and clanging around. He never means to cause accidents, though, and often says sorry, explaining that it was "a slip of the hook!"

Together Kevin and Victor make a Really Useful team, ready to help any engine get back on the rails as quickly as possible.

Really Useful Facts

Paintwork: Yellow with yellow and black hazard stripes

Wheels: 4

Steam or diesel crane? Diesel

Jobs: Repairing engines who come to the Steamworks

Friends: Victor and Spencer

Kevin likes: Working with Victor, who has a lot to teach him

Kevin doesn't like: Getting in trouble for dropping things!

BUST MY BUFFERS!

Kevin helped repair Hiro and made him look splendid from funnel to footplate!

LADY HATT

All About Lady Hatt

A kind and gentle woman, **Lady Jane Hatt** is married to Sir Topham Hatt.

She doesn't call him "Sir Topham Hatt" as the engines do, though—she calls him "Topham"!

Lady Hatt sometimes helps her husband with railway business, and the engines have loved helping throw parties for her birthday over the years.

Lady Hatt likes railway life and talking to the engines, but she didn't like Annie and Clarabel until they were cleaned and given a fresh coat of paint. Now she is happy to travel as a passenger in either of Thomas' two coaches.

Really Useful Facts

Friends: Sir Topham Hatt, Sodor's Steam Engines

Grandchildren: Stephen and Bridget

Lady Hatt loves: The engines, and praises them when they've been Really Useful

Lady Hatt doesn't like: Dirty or old-fashioned coaches

BUST MY BUFFERS!

Although her husband runs a railway, Lady Hatt also likes a day out on a boat or in their blue car.

MAVIS

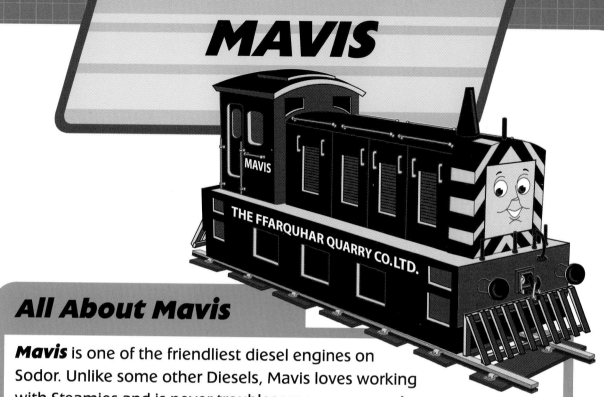

All About Mavis

Mavis is one of the friendliest diesel engines on Sodor. Unlike some other Diesels, Mavis loves working with Steamies and is never troublesome on purpose!

Mavis used to spend most of her time with Toby, Bill, and Ben at the old quarry, but now she works at the Sodor Slate Quarry. Brave, honest, and hardworking, Mavis would love to work on the Main Line if given the chance.

Like Toby's, Mavis' six wheels are covered by a cowcatcher and sideplates so she can run near public roads.

Mavis has her name and the words "The Ffarquhar Quarry Co. Ltd." painted in white on her sides.

Really Useful Facts

Paintwork: Black with yellow and black hazard stripes

Steam or diesel engine? Diesel

Wheels: 6

Mavis pulls: Trucks at Sodor's quarries

Friends: Toby, Bill, and Ben

Mavis loves: Cheering up steam engines if they are sad

Mavis doesn't like: Diesel and his naughty tricks!

BUST MY BUFFERS!

Mavis once tried to leave the quarry but caused an accident for Toby. Since then, she has always done as she is told.

MR. PERCIVAL

All About Mr. Percival

Mr. Percival is in charge of the Narrow Gauge Railway on the Island of Sodor. He is kind to his engines, and together they run a Really Useful rail service in the center of the island.

Like Sir Topham Hatt, Mr. Percival dresses very stylishly in a suit and yellow waistcoat. He also wears glasses and a bowler hat.

Mr. Percival doesn't much like cars and prefers to ride his trusty bicycle to work and back.

Really Useful Facts

Clothes: A stylish suit, a bowler hat, and glasses

Jobs: Looking after the Narrow Gauge Railway and the engines who work there

Friends: Sir Topham Hatt and his engines

Mr. Percival loves: To ride his favorite bicycle

Mr. Percival doesn't like: When engines or trucks cause confusion and delay

BUST MY BUFFERS!

Mr. Percival has a wife named Polly and five children!

OLIVER the Great Western Engine

All About Oliver

Oliver is a Great Western tank engine who proudly works on Duck's branch line. He has two coaches and a brake van called Toad.

A long time ago, Oliver ran away with Isabel and Toad because he was afraid he was going to be scrapped. They hid between signal boxes until Douglas came to their rescue. Oliver's paint had faded by the time he was rescued, leaving him a rusty red color. After his rescue, he was repainted green and has remained so ever since.

Really Useful Facts

Number: 11

Paintwork: Green

Tender? No

Wheels: 6

Steam or diesel engine? Steam

Oliver pulls: His coaches, Isabel and Dulcie, and a brake van called Toad

Friends: Douglas and Duck

Oliver loves: His Great Western colors

BUST MY BUFFERS!

When Oliver arrived on Sodor, he didn't know how to handle trucks, and he fell down a turntable well!

PETER SAM

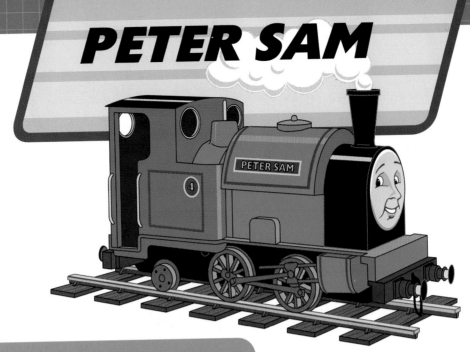

All About Peter Sam

Peter Sam works on Mr. Percival's Narrow Gauge Railway. A happy and kind engine, Peter Sam doesn't mind extra work and is polite to coaches and trucks alike. Passengers are always pleased when he takes them on rides up and down the mountain tracks, too.

When Peter Sam first arrived on the railway, he was called Stuart after the engineer who made him. He likes being called Peter Sam these days and thinks it suits him much better. Don't you?

Really Useful Facts

Number: 4

Paintwork: Green with a red buffer beam

Tender? No

Wheels: 6

Steam or diesel engine? Steam

Peter Sam pulls: Coaches and trucks

Friends: Sir Handel and Duncan

Peter Sam loves: All kinds of work, including pulling trucks who never play tricks on him!

Peter Sam doesn't like: Winter — when there are icicles!

BUST MY BUFFERS!

Once, Peter Sam's funnel hit an icicle, and he had to get a new one. While he was waiting, he used a rusty pipe as a funnel!

RHENEAS

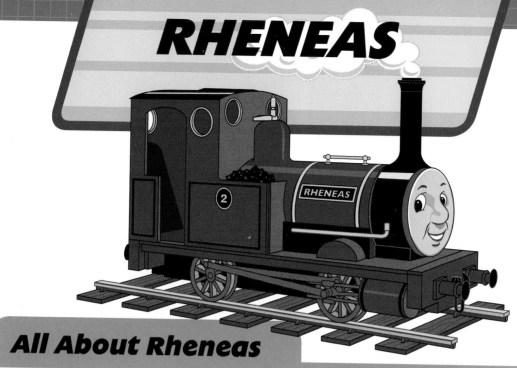

All About Rheneas

Rheneas is one of the oldest engines on the Island of Sodor and works on the Narrow Gauge Railway. He is a tough little engine, but because of his age, he often breaks down. Rheneas still works hard, though, to make sure that the passengers know just how fine a railway the Narrow Gauge Railway is!

Rheneas enjoys doing kind things to help his friends, like the time he decided to take Skarloey's coal trucks to the wharf as a surprise for him.

Really Useful Facts

Number: 2

Paintwork: Dark red with black and gold

Tender? No

Wheels: 4

Steam or diesel engine? Steam

Rheneas pulls: Mainly passenger trains

Friends: Skarloey, Rusty, and Duncan

Rheneas loves: Working on the Narrow Gauge Railway

Rheneas doesn't like: Breaking down

BUST MY BUFFERS!

Did you know that Rheneas is a hero? He once saved Skarloey from a landslide.

ROCKY the Rescue Crane

All About Rocky

Rocky is the gentle giant of Sodor. He is a very strong crane who wants to be everyone's best friend. With his rotating crane arm, Rocky does the heavy lifting on the island—jobs like picking up derailed engines and getting them back on track!

When Rocky first arrived on Sodor, Gordon didn't believe that a crane with no engine could lift a large tender engine like himself, but Rocky soon proved him wrong!

Now Rocky is an important member of the Sodor Search and Rescue Team with his friends Captain and Harold. If ever there is an accident, Rocky will come to the rescue!

Really Useful Facts

Paintwork: Burgundy with yellow hazard stripes

Steam or diesel crane? Steam

Jobs: Heavy lifting and getting engines back on the rails

Friends: Harold and Captain

Rocky loves: Coming to the rescue of anyone in danger

Rocky doesn't like: There's nothing that bothers Rocky!

BUST MY BUFFERS!

Rocky has no engine of his own and must ask other engines to pull him to wherever he is needed.

ROSIE

All About Rosie

Rosie is a small purple tank engine who has lots of pretty freckles on her face.

Rosie wants to be like Thomas—a Really Useful Engine! She likes to follow him everywhere and copy everything he does!

Once, Sir Topham Hatt asked Rosie to be Emily's back engine, but Rosie naughtily set off with the Funfair Special all by herself. She thought she was doing Emily a favor, but instead she caused confusion and delay when the trucks came loose. Rosie had to fetch Rocky to repair the damage before she and Emily could pull the train together.

Really Useful Facts

Paintwork: Purple with gray side tanks and red wheels

Tender? No

Wheels: 6

Steam or diesel engine? Steam

Rosie pulls: Trucks

Best friend: Thomas

Rosie loves: Racing through puddles with Thomas!

Rosie doesn't like: Being a back engine

BUST MY BUFFERS!

Once, Rosie rescued Thomas after he had splashed through a puddle and put out his fire.

RUSTY

All About Rusty

Rusty is the only diesel engine on the Narrow Gauge Railway. He was brought to work there to help Sir Handel and Peter Sam while Skarloey was away being repaired.

Rusty works hard each day to finish all of his jobs, which include pulling trains of workmen and equipment when he's told to, though he spends most of his time helping to maintain the line.

Rusty loves adventure and is one of the kinder Diesels on the island. He especially loves sounding his two-toned horn when he passes his friends!

Really Useful Facts

Number: Rusty is number 5 on the Narrow Gauge Railway.

Paintwork: Rusty orange with his name and number painted in white

Tender? No

Wheels: 4

Steam or diesel engine? Diesel

Rusty pulls: Goods and passenger trains

Friends: Sir Handel, Peter Sam, and Stepney

Rusty loves: His two-toned horn!

Rusty doesn't like: Waiting — Rusty is always in a hurry.

BUST MY BUFFERS!

Unlike some of the diesel engines, Rusty would never want any Steamie to be scrapped. He once rescued Stepney when his Steamie friend was in trouble.

SALTY the
Dockside Diesel

All About Salty

Salty is a weather-worn Diesel who works at Brendam Docks. He loves the sea more than anything, and loves to tell tales of his life by the ocean waves to anyone who'll listen! At first, Bill and Ben didn't like his stories, but now they love a good tale in the sheds at night. Cranky isn't so fond of the stories, though!

When Salty first arrived on Sodor, he had to work at the quarry in the middle of the island and really missed seeing the sea. Now Salty spends his days at the docks and loves his work there.

Really Useful Facts

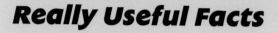

Number: 2991

Paintwork: Red with yellow and black hazard stripes

Wheels: 6

Steam or diesel engine? Diesel

Salty pulls: Cargo and trucks. It's a mystery how he gets the trucks to behave!

Friends: Steamies and Diesels alike!

Salty loves: Telling stories and singing sea shanties

Salty doesn't like: Being away from the sea for too long

BUST MY BUFFERS!

When Salty told Thomas a tale about buried treasure on Sodor, Thomas followed Salty's clues and found a hidden chest!

SIR HANDEL

All About Sir Handel

Sir Handel is one of the oldest engines on the Narrow Gauge Railway. He thinks that he knows best and should be in charge of the other engines, which sometimes gets him into trouble.

When he arrived on Sodor, Sir Handel had many adventures. He was derailed by his own coaches when he stopped too quickly in front of some sheep. Another time, he had an argument with George the Steamroller and George smashed into Sir Handel's trucks!

These days, he is an older and wiser engine, but he's still a bit too big for his buffers.

Really Useful Facts

Number: 3

Paintwork: Blue with red lining and a red buffer beam

Wheels: 6

Steam or diesel engine? Steam

Sir Handel pulls: Coaches — stubborn Sir Handel often refuses to pull trucks.

Friends: Peter Sam and the other Narrow Gauge engines

Sir Handel doesn't like: Being sent to the sheds by himself

BUST MY BUFFERS!

Sir Handel used to be called Falcon but was renamed when he came to work on the Narrow Gauge Railway.

SIR TOPHAM HATT

All About Sir Topham Hatt

Sir Topham Hatt is a very important man indeed. He's in charge of the main railway on the Island of Sodor, so he has a lot of engines, coaches, crew, and passengers to look after.

Sir Topham Hatt is firm but fair and always speaks kindly to the engines if they are upset. He soon reminds them who's in charge if they try to cause mischief, though!

Sir Topham Hatt's wife is Lady Hatt. He has two grandchildren, Stephen and Bridget, who love to visit the engines.

Really Useful Facts

Clothes: Sir Topham Hatt is always well dressed in his suit and tie, yellow waistcoat, and shiny top hat!

Jobs: Running the railway and looking after his engines and their crews and passengers. Checking timetables.

Friends: Everyone on Sodor loves Sir Topham Hatt!

Sir Topham Hatt loves: Trains that run on time — he wants all his passengers to think he runs a Really Useful Railway.

Sir Topham Hatt doesn't like: Engines who are too big for their buffers!

BUST MY BUFFERS!

Did you know that Sir Topham Hatt used to be an engineer? He doesn't mind getting his hands dirty if an engine needs mending.

SKARLOEY

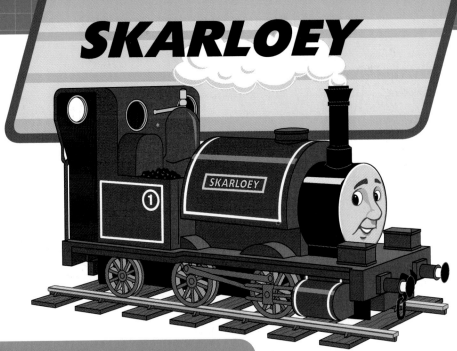

All About Skarloey

Skarloey is another old engine who works on the Narrow Gauge Railway. He is painted red with white stripes, and has the number 1, as well as a nameplate, on both sides.

When Skarloey first came to Sodor, he wasn't very good at doing as he was told and refused to pull trucks.

Skarloey had to go away for a long time to be mended, leaving Rheneas to run the mountain line on his own until Sir Handel and Peter Sam arrived to help. He returned to the railway a stronger and wiser engine.

Really Useful Facts

Number: 1

Paintwork: Dark red with white lining

Wheels: 6

Steam or diesel engine? Steam

Skarloey pulls: Mainly coaches

Friends: Rheneas, Sir Handel, Peter Sam, and Rusty

Skarloey loves: Racing with Rheneas

Skarloey doesn't like: Rickety bridges and stormy weather

BUST MY BUFFERS!

Rheneas, who looks very like Skarloey, once rescued Skarloey when he was caught in a mudslide.

SPENCER

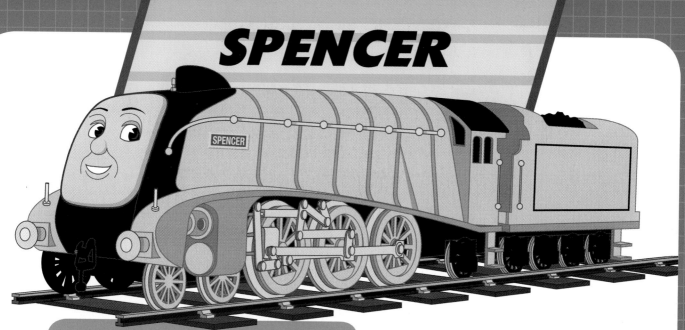

All About Spencer

Spencer pulls the private train when the Duke and Duchess of Boxford visit Sodor. He's a sleek silver engine who likes to show just how fast he can go. At first, the other engines were impressed by Spencer's speed and strength, but later they found out that he was too big for his buffers!

Spencer always thinks that he knows best. Once, he didn't listen to Gordon, who warned him to take on more water, and soon ran out of steam and pretended he had a leaky tank to cover his mistake!

Really Useful Facts

Paintwork: Silver

Tender: Yes

Wheels: 12 with 8 on his tender

Steam or diesel engine? Steam

Spencer pulls: The Duke and Duchess of Boxford's private train

Friends: Spencer doesn't make friends easily because he's so boastful.

Spencer loves: Thundering down the line as fast as he can!

Spencer doesn't like: Big engines who are just as fast as he is

BUST MY BUFFERS!

Take a closer look at Spencer and you'll see that he doesn't have a dome!

STEPNEY
the Bluebell Engine

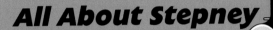

All About Stepney

Stepney is a tank engine who once sat lost on a siding. When the Bluebell line needed an engine, Rusty passed the siding and saved him from being scrapped. Then Sir Topham Hatt brought Stepney to work on the North Western Railway.

Stepney had another close call when he took a trip to help Toby and Mavis at the quarry. On his way home, he became lost in the dark, and 'Arry and Bert tried to scrap him into pieces.

Now Stepney is very pleased to be working again and loves long runs on the country lines. He's a friendly engine who doesn't even mind pulling trucks!

Really Useful Facts

Number: 55

Paintwork: Gold with green and red trim

Wheels: 6

Steam or diesel engine? Steam

Stepney pulls: Coaches and trucks

Friends: Rusty and the Narrow Gauge Engines

Stepney loves: Long-distance journeys

Stepney doesn't like: 'Arry and Bert and the Smelters' Yard

BUST MY BUFFERS!

Stepney once caught a ball in one of his trucks when passing Elsbridge Cricket Club!

TROUBLESOME TRUCKS

All About the Troublesome Trucks

The **Troublesome Trucks** are the chief mischief-makers on the island. Some engines call them the "Rascals of the Railway" because they are so naughty and silly.

It's an engine's job to make sure the noisy trucks do as they are told. They love to sing songs and play tricks on the engines, bumping and shoving them.

The Troublesome Trucks are often the cause of accidents on the island, and don't seem to mind being damaged and coming off the rails.

Really Useful Facts

Paintwork: The trucks are made out of wood and painted gray.

Wheels: 4 each

Jobs: Working at the quarries, the yards, and docks on Sodor. They carry all sorts of Useful loads!

Friends: Each other and the naughtier diesel engines on Sodor

The trucks love: Causing trouble for engines — particularly Steamies!

BUST MY BUFFERS!

Edward, Salty, and Stepney are the best engines for keeping trucks out of trouble.

VICTOR

All About Victor

Victor is the manager of the Sodor Steamworks. He is a very busy engine, always on the run — fixing broken-down engines, finding new parts, and trying to keep his assistant, Kevin, out of trouble!

Victor is a wise and friendly engine who is always ready to help his friends, but he refuses to put up with any nonsense from engines like Spencer.

Victor has a heart of gold and a good sense of humor. All the engines know just how Useful he is — it is Victor who keeps the Island of Sodor steaming along!

Really Useful Facts

Paintwork: Dark red with yellow stripes, and black and yellow hazard stripes on his buffer beams

Tender? No

Wheels: 4

Steam or diesel engine? Steam

Jobs: Fixing engines and other vehicles that need repair

Best friend: Kevin

Victor loves: Being in charge of the Steamworks and mending engines who need his help

Victor doesn't like: Kevin's clumsiness!

BUST MY BUFFERS!

The side of Victor's cab carries the badge of the Sodor Steamworks, where he proudly works.